THE CALL
OF THE
SHOFAR

AND OTHER STORIES

BY
NISSAN MINDEL

ADAPTED BY
CHANA ZUBER-SHARFSTEIN

ILLUSTRATED BY
ZALMAN KLEINMAN

Our Acknowledgment

To the TALKS and TALES, monthly magazine, published by Merkos
L'Inyonei Chinuch, for permission to use the stories in this volume.

Published by
MERKOS L'INYONEI CHINUCH, Inc.
770 Eastern Parkway
Brooklyn, N. Y. 11213
HYacinth 3-9250-1

נדפס בדפוס האחים גרויס

Printed in U.S.A. GROSS BROS. Printing Co. Inc.

Contents

THE CALL OF
THE SHOFAR

HIS is the story of a shofar and a little boy called Moshe.

Do you know what a shofar is?

A shofar is made of the horn of a ram, the male sheep.

On Rosh Hashonoh, the New Year, wherever Jews are, all over the world, the shofar is blown.

The sound of the shofar reminds us that we are Jews.

The shofar calls us to ask forgiveness for all the wrong things we have done.

The Baal-shem-tov said that the sounding of the shofar was like the sad cry of someone lost in the woods.

The sound of the shofar is like a lost child crying, "Oh, father, my father. Please help me."

Once upon a time, many years ago, in the faraway country of Russia, there lived a poor boy called Moshe. He had neither father nor mother. When he was small everybody called him Moshele, which means Little Moshe.

He went to "cheder" with all the other children in his little town. He liked to learn "chumash" and "gemorah." When he became a bit older, he had to go to work. Poor Moshele had no father or mother to take care of him. He wanted to stay in Yeshiva and learn, and maybe some day become a big scholar. But Moshele had no choice. He was a poor orphan. He had to get a job and learn to take care of himself.

Moshele decided to become a peddler. In those days

there weren't many stores. Peddlers travelled all over the country with suitcases full of things to sell. Moshele got a suitcase and filled it with all kinds of odds and ends. He had needles and thread, scissors, thimbles, pieces of material, all sorts of buttons, and many other things.

It was not easy to be a peddler. In the summertime it was hot, and Moshele became tired and thirsty walking on the dusty country roads with his heavy suitcase. In the wintertime, Moshele shivered and froze because his clothes were not warm enough to protect him from the icy winds.

And so his life went on until one day poor Moshele was caught in a very big snow storm. It was a real blizzard. Snow was falling and falling from the grey skies.

Everything was covered with a thick blanket of snow. Moshele tried to be brave and cheerful. He kept his spirits up by reciting by heart all the Psalms he knew. With each step it was getting more and more difficult to walk. His suitcase felt heavier and heavier. The snow was up to his ankles. Soon the snow was almost up to his knees.

Moshele could hardly move with his big heavy suitcase. Snow was everywhere. It was difficult to follow the road because the snow covered everything. Without knowing it, Moshele walked off the road and into the

woods. He was very, very tired. When he found a stump of a tree, he decided to sit down and rest for awhile. Moshele knew it would be dangerous if he fell asleep. He tried very hard to stay awake. He kept saying to himself over and over again: "Do not fall asleep. You must stay awake. If you fall asleep you might freeze to death." Moshele was so very, very tired and he thought a short rest would be good for him. He was shivering in his thin old clothes, and he felt very sleepy.

Suddenly he began to feel warm and comfortable. He thought that he was sitting near a cosy, bright fire. He stretched out his hands and feet to warm himself near the fire. For a moment Moshele felt as if sharp needles were pricking his finger tips. Soon that stopped, and Moshele felt happy and relaxed. The flames of the fire blazed ever more brightly. . . .

It was beginning to become dark outside. Soon it would be night. The peasant on the road with his horse and sled was happy he would soon be home. But wait!!! What was that? Away from the road, somewhat into the woods, he noticed something odd. What was it? It looked like a human being lying in the snow. Could it be alive? Was it really a human being? He stopped his horse, and ran over to take a better look. He could hardly believe his eyes. It was a young boy. He brushed the snow off his clothes. There was no sign of life. The body was almost frozen stiff.

There was not a moment to be wasted. Maybe he could still save the life of the young boy. Quickly the peasant pulled out his knife and began to cut the stiff, frozen clothing off the still body. Then he started to rub the boy's body with some snow. He rubbed him as fast as he could. He rubbed him hard. As soon as the snow melted from the rubbing, he picked up another handful and continued his work. He looked at the boy to see if there was any sign of life. But nothing changed. The peasant was afraid to stop even though he was getting tired from rubbing the boy's body with snow.

All of a sudden, the boy stirred. He moved only slightly, but the peasant felt happy. He knew the blood had begun to flow again in the boy's young body and the

worst danger was over. The peasant carried the boy to his sled and covered him with some warm blankets. Then he drove his horse and sled as fast as he could to his farm in a village nearby.

The peasant brought the boy into the house. He put him down on some blankets near the fireplace. He rubbed the boy's body again with some snow until he saw the skin begin to glow and look healthy. The peasant warmed up some milk and fed the boy slowly with a spoon. Moshele opened his eyes for a moment. Then he closed them again and went to sleep.

He slept peacefully all night. In the morning, the crow of the rooster woke him up. Moshele opened his eyes and looked all around. Everything seemed strange. He could not understand where he ws. He tried to remember what had happened, but Moshele had forgotten everything. He could not remember his home. He could not remember his travels as a peddler. But he was too tired to think. All he wanted now was to sleep.

When Moshele woke up, he felt as if someone were sticking pins and needles into him. That is how you feel when you are frostbitten, you know. You feel as if someone were pricking you all over with pins and needles.

The peasant's wife came to Moshele to greet him. "How do you feel?" she asked in Russian, for this story happened in Russia. "I guess I feel alright, thank you," answered Moshele. He was still wondering what had happened to him and how he had come to the peasant's home.

The woman prepared some hot cereal for Moshele and fed him slowly with a spoon. "What is your name?" she asked him. Moshele became frightened. He could not remember his own name! He tried to think as hard as he could, but he just could not remember. Moshele had been very sick. He had almost frozen to death. Now he was beginning to feel stronger, but he remembered nothing.

"I don't know. I can't remember my name," he said sadly.

"Never mind," said the peasant woman. "Don't worry about that. You can stay with us in our home. We'll call you Peter. How about that?" and she gave him a kind smile. Moshele smiled back at her. "Yes," he said, "it would be fine."

Moshele, or Peter as he was called now, lived in the home of the peasant and his wife and became a part of their family. He did not remember that he was a Jewish boy and did not belong in that house. He forgot all about the Jewish way of life and became very much like the farmer and his wife.

All summer long, Peter helped with the work on the farm. He ploughed the fields and made nice, even rows. He sowed the seeds. He watched everything grow. Peter was not a lazy boy. He worked hard, and the farmer was

very pleased with him. Peter was a capable boy and a good worker.

When fall came, it was time to reap the harvest. One autumn day, the farmer said to Peter, "Tomorrow we will drive into town. We will take some of our products to the market to sell." Peter was very excited. The work on the farm was hard and Peter had been very busy. It would be great fun to go into town.

Peter was so happy, he could hardly sleep that night.

The trip to town was not very long, but Peter thought it seemed like hours. When they got into town, they were very surprised. There were no people on the streets. The little town looked deserted.

When they passed by the little shul in the town, they saw it was filled with people. Everyone had come to shul to pray because it was Rosh Hashonoh. The peasant decided that they should drive back to the farm because it was not a good time for business. Peter kept looking at the shul. He did not want to return to the farm. He could not tear himself away from the shul. He begged the peasant to stay in town for awhile. The peasant saw how excited Peter was. He said Peter could spend the afternoon by himself looking around the town. After all, Peter deserved a treat after his hard work on the farm.

Peter felt as if someone were pulling him toward the shul. He was not thinking. He felt as if he was sleep-walking. Without knowing that he had walked there, he suddenly found himself at the entrance to the shul. The men were wrapped in their prayer shawls. Everyone was praying and some were weeping. No one even noticed Peter standing near the door. No one paid any attention to him.

Peter looked all around. Somehow it all seemed familiar to him. Had he ever been here before? His heart began to beat faster. The tune and melodies of the cantor were familiar to him. The scrolls of the Torah that were being carried out of the Ark were familiar. And he was beginning to hear the words in the prayers and they sounded familiar too. Slowly his memory was returning to him and everything in the shul brought back fresh, new memories. As if glued to the spot, Peter stood motionless and stared. . . .

Peter did not know how long he had been standing there when he began to notice a feeling of excitement among the worshippers in the shul. Everyone was becoming very quiet. There was finally complete silence in the crowd. All the people stood still in their places. Peter hardly dared to breathe. It seemed as if the air was filled with holiness. Peter closed his eyes for a moment, and he felt as if angels were all around him.

Suddenly the silence was shattered by the loud blast

of the shofar. The old cantor was blowing the shofar. The sound of the shofar made Peter feel very strange. As each note was blown and moved upward, Peter felt as if he had wings and was flying upward with it.

Peter's eyes filled with tears. The tears began rolling down his cheeks. But inside, in his heart, Peter was smiling. Everything was now clear to him. "Moshele, you are a Jew," the shofar called. "Moshele, you are a Jew."

And Moshele said quietly, "Thank you, shofar. Oh, thank you, thank you. Thank you for helping me find my way. Thank you for reminding me that I am a Jew.".

THE MIRROR

HIS is the story about a very beautiful and very special mirror. It hung on a wall in the dining room of a fine house belonging to a rich man.

The mirror was large and square-shaped. All around it there was a wide, thick gold frame carved with beautiful designs of leaves and flowers. Everyone that saw the mirror admired it, but everyone also noticed that it was imperfect. On one of the corners, you see, the silver backing had been scraped off so that this part of the mirror looked like plain glass. People would remark upon its beauty and then say, "Oh, what a pity! Too bad the mirror is damaged." To everyone's surprise the owner would tell his visitors that it was he himself who had scraped the silver backing off on purpose! Can you imagine owning such a costly mirror, a work of art, and then ruining it? But let me tell you the story of that mirror.

Many years ago in Poland there lived a Jewish man called Abraham. He owned a small store and he earned just enough money to take care of his family. He was not a rich man, but he also was not a very, very poor man. He had only a few customers. Sometimes people left without buying anything because Abraham did not have many things to choose from. They went to the big stores instead where they could find what they wanted.

Abraham was happy with his life. He never complained. And even though he was not rich, he always had enough to share with others. No visitor that came to his home ever left hungry. Every time a poor person needed help, Abraham always found money to give him. No one knew that Abraham and his wife often gave away their own portion of the meal so that the stranger should not be hungry. Money that was set aside for buying clothes or fixing the house often was given away to poor people. Abraham was a kind and good man, and always felt sorry for others.

And so he lived a very simple life. His home was small. The house really needed a paint job, but there was never enough money for that. It seemed to Abraham that it was more important to help someone in real trouble than to paint a house. His furniture was old for the same reason. The curtains on the windows had probably been washed a hundred times. Abraham and his wife had no carpets on their floor. Their clothes were plain, and they did not often buy new things. Many of their cups and plates had chips and cracks. The food they ate was simple.

Yes, it was not a very fancy home. But it was a real home. It was a warm and happy place. Everyone felt comfortable and relaxed there. Abraham had many visitors because everyone knew that he was kind and liked to be helpful.

One day Abraham was standing in the doorway of his little store waiting for customers. Suddenly he noticed a stranger walking toward his store. Abraham lived in a small town so he knew all the people there. When the stranger was near the store, Abraham asked him how he could help. "Maybe you would like to come to my home and rest awhile," he said. "If you are hungry, please be my guest. If you are thirsty, please come with me for something to drink. Perhaps you need money? We will help you."

Abraham's invitation was so warm and friendly that the stranger decided to stop in his house for a rest.

What Abraham did not know was that this was no ordinary stranger. This was a very holy, wise and famous Rebbe from a town far way. He was on his way to a wedding and happened to pass through Abraham's town. The Rebbe was an important man and many people in Poland travelled long distances to listen to his words of wisdom, or to ask for a blessing or prayer in time of need. It would have been a great honor for any home to have this Rebbe as a guest.

The Rebbe soon noticed that Abraham was not a rich man. He saw that the home was simple. Everything in this home looked old and worn. But he also saw that Abraham was a very kindhearted man. He knew many rich people who could have helped the poor much more easily than Abraham, but who did much less than he. Abraham did more than his share in hospitality to visitors — *Hachnosas Orchim* — and the giving of charity — *Tzedoko.* The Rebbe enjoyed his short stay. Abraham and his wife did everything they could to please him and make him comfortable. The Rebbe was pleased to have met such a fine Jewish couple. He blessed Abraham with

riches—Parnosso—so that he should be able to continue helping the poor and needy more easily.

After the Rebbe left, Abraham's store suddenly became a very busy place. All day long customers were coming in. Everyone found what he wanted, and no longer did people leave his store to shop somewhere else. With each day that passed, Abraham had more new customers and more money to bring home. Soon he had to make his store larger to fit all his new customers. After awhile, Abraham became a very big, important and rich storekeeper. He became one of the richest men in the

whole town. The Rebbe's blessing that Abraham should become wealthy had come true.

To be rich seems mighty good when one is poor. People sometimes think that if they were rich, life would be beautiful. But being rich can be a problem too. Now that Abraham had a big store, he had a lot more work to do. He worried about robbers breaking into his store or home. He worried about his business. He wanted his store to keep on growing and become bigger and bigger. He wanted a very beautiful home. He wanted new, fancy clothes. Because Abraham was busy with his store, he found less and less time for learning Torah and going to Shul to pray. He did not even have time to bother with poor people. Abraham could only be seen by special appointment. His secretaries were told to give money to needy people who came for his help, that is true, but

Abraham had no time to listen to their stories or problems.

Abraham and his wife built a brand new house that almost looked like a palace. It had many rooms, and all the rooms were large and beautiful. On the windows hung soft velvet drapes. The floors were covered with thick rugs. There was wallpaper on the walls. The kitchen was filled with new pots and pans. There were lots of fine dishes in the cabinets. All the furniture was new and expensive. The dining room table was made of shiny wood. The chairs in the living room were soft and plump. On the walls hung paintings by real artists. And on one wall in the living room there hung a huge mirror. It was so big it almost covered the whole wall. All around this mirror there was a wide, thick frame of gold. No one else in the town had such a fine mirror. Everyone that saw it spoke of its beauty. It really was a masterpiece.

There were many servants in this new house. Abraham and his wife wore the finest clothes. They ate the best kinds of food. But this house was so fancy, they did not want to let beggars or poor people come in. Strangers were no longer invited for a meal. Servants would open the door and give some money to the needy, but that was all.

"Abraham is different," people said. "He has changed since he became rich. What a pity! He was always so kind and good, and now look at him. He has no time for any of us any more." And they would shake their heads sadly and remember the good old times when Abraham had never been too busy to help others.

Time passed. One day a messenger came to visit Abraham. He had been sent a long distance from the famous Rebbe who had given Abraham the blessing of riches. The news of Abraham's good fortune had reached the ears of the Rebbe and now he needed his help. An innocent Jewish man had been put in prison on false charges and a great deal of money was needed for his ransom. It was a case of *Pidyon Shvuim*. Of course Abraham was happy to help. He gave the messenger the money and sent him off with good wishes for a safe trip home. He also sent regards to the Rebbe.

The messenger had completed his job, but he did not feel happy. It had been difficult for him to speak to Abraham in person. His secretaries had not wanted to let a stranger into Abraham's private office. Abraham had given him the money, but he had not invited him to his home for some food or rest. The messenger was surprised. The Rebbe had praised Abraham and often spoken of his hospitality and charitable ways. The messenger could not understand what had happened.

When he came back to the Rebbe, he gave him the money and told him everything about his trip. The Rebbe shook his head sadly. He understood that Abraham, the poor man, had a heart of gold, but Abraham, the rich man, with all his gold, seemed to have a heart more like stone.

The Rebbe decided to visit Abraham to see what could be done.

When the Rebbe arrived at Abraham's house, Abraham welcomed him warmly and invited him into his home.

This house looked very different from the home that Abraham had lived in when the Rebbe first visited him.

The house was big and beautiful, but gone was the friendliness and warmth one had felt in the simple, old home. The Rebbe walked on the heavy rug. He saw the costly paintings. He looked at the expensive, new furniture. The house seemed freshly painted. The drapes were made from the finest, softest velvet. And then he noticed the mirror. He looked at its shiny gold frame. It was the biggest mirror he had ever seen.

"Quite a change, is it not?" said Abraham with a pleased smile on his face. "And that mirror," he continued, "is my favorite treasure. Of all the lovely things I own, I like that mirror the best. It cost a great deal of money, but it was worth it. It is truly a masterpiece, a work of art, is it not?" he said and turned to the Rebbe.

"Yes," the Rebbe answered. "Quite a change. Quite a change." He said this softly, in a low, serious voice, and his face looked sad. He said the same thing that Abraham had said, but he meant something very different. He was thinking of the change in Abraham and this made him unhappy.

Suddenly the Rebbe thought of something. "Come here," he called to Abraham. And he asked him to walk over to the mirror and stand in front of it. The Rebbe then walked away a bit and asked Abraham what he saw.

Abraham was puzzled at this, but answered, "Myself. That is what I see in this mirror. My own reflection. That is all I can see."

"Look closely," the Rebbe said, "what else do you see?"

"I see my lovely furniture reflected in the mirror. I see my paintings. I see my rugs and drapes. I can see many things in my beautiful home," answered Abraham.

The Rebbe then walked over to the window with Abraham. He pushed aside the velvet drapes and told Abraham to look out into the street. Abraham's home was on a big street, and people were always passing by. Since it was a small town, Abraham knew almost all the people

walking past his house. The Rebbe asked him many questions about all the people they saw. And Abraham told him that the woman with the basket was a poor widow with many small children. She was hoping that kind people would put food in the basket for her family. He told the Rebbe about Bentze, the water-carrier, who was getting old and found it hard to carry the water. He pointed out Yankel the Tailor, a fine Jew who went to shul every day, but was very poor and never had enough money for his family.

Abraham was wondering why the Rebbe was asking him all these questions. The Rebbe was a serious man who never had time to waste. Why should he be so curious about all these people? Abraham was very surprised.

Then the Rebbe said to Abraham, "It is strange, is it not, that a mirror and a window are both made of glass and yet they are very different."

"What do you mean?" asked Abraham.

"Well," said the Rebbe, "when you looked in the mirror you could only see yourself and all the things that belong to you. You could see much more when you looked out the window. Then you could see all your neighbors and friends from the whole town."

"That is true," said Abraham. "A mirror and a window are both made from glass. The window is transparent. Light can pass right through it. It is clear and you can see everything through it. The mirror is covered with silver on one side. The rays of light cannot pass through, and therefore a mirror can only reflect what is in front of it."

"I see," said the Rebbe and nodded his head. "I see. The piece of glass that is plain is clear through and through. When it is covered with silver, it becomes darkened on one side and then you can see only yourself. Hm, very interesting. It is really quite fantastic and wonderful, isn't it? Now do you think it will work the other way too? Could you take a mirror and scrape off the silver so that you would be able to see everyone else instead of yourself?"

No wonder so many people loved this Rebbe. He was a very wise and holy man. Finally, Abraham was beginning to understand everything that had happened to him since he became rich.

Abraham's eyes filled with tears. He felt so ashamed. He had been blessed with riches, and instead of helping the poor more, he had done less than when he was a poor man.

Abraham understood what the Rebbe meant. When he was a little storekeeper, he had been like the plain piece of glass, the glass in the window. He had seen everyone else and thought of everyone else. There had always been time to help the needy. When he became rich, he was just like the mirror. Covered with silver, like the mirror, he had only been able to see himself. The mirror showed him his own reflection and stopped him from seeing what was happening outside.

He knew that he had disappointed the Rebbe. He

was unworthy of the blessing he had received from him. Abraham felt deeply ashamed. "Help me," he begged the Rebbe. "Tell me what I should do. Please, please help me."

The Rebbe told Abraham that he must return to his old life of hospitality. He should remember the poor and needy and be kind to them more than ever. The Rebbe further told Abraham that he was to fulfill the Mitzvah of Tzedoko with the same devotion that he had practised this Mitzvah in poverty. His riches would then become a blessing for him and all the people in the little town.

Abraham listened carefully to each word the Rebbe said. That same evening, he made a big party in his home. The whole town was invited, especially all the poor people. Everyone had a fine time.

Then Abraham asked for silence. He made a short speech and asked for everyone's forgiveness. He told his guests that he was sorry for the way he had acted after he became rich. His life would now be different. He promised them that his doors would always be open for everyone, and that he never would be too busy to help those that needed him. The guests clapped their hands. They were truly happy. Everyone had missed Abraham's warm and friendly ways. It was good to know that Abraham would be his good old self again.

Abraham never wanted to forget his promise. He never wanted to become cold and unkind again.

After all the guests had left, he walked over to his beautiful mirror, the treasure that he liked most of all. With a sharp knife he scraped off the silver covering in one corner. He did not stop until that part was as clear as glass. Only then was he satisfied.

And for the rest of his life that mirror reminded Abraham of the true meaning of the Mitzvoth of Tzedoko and Hachnosas Orchim—Charity and Hospitality to visitors.

THE BRIDE

EVERYONE loves to go to a wedding. There is so much joy and excitement. The band plays lively, gay tunes, and the men and women dance on the opposite sides of the mechitza (partition). There is such a large selection of things to eat, one does not know what to taste first. Sometimes there is chopped liver shaped like a bird. The fruit platters are very colorful. There are yellow chunks of pineapple, red balls of watermelon, green balls of honeydew, and slices of oranges and tangerines. The cake platters make your mouth water. There are lemon cakes, cakes with white frosting, and cakes with chocolate frosting. The cookies come in many shapes and are nicely decorated. And all the guests smile and look happy in their best Shabbos clothes.

Prettiest of all is, of course always, the bride, the kallah. She sits high up on a chair that looks like a throne. Even if you know the kallah well, she seems special or different on the day of her wedding. There is a certain glow about her. With her beautiful white gown and the veil covering her hair, she looks like a real princess. Every kallah becomes a beauty on the day of her wedding. One can feel and see her happiness and joy, and that is what makes weddings the best kind of parties.

Zlata was a young, beautiful kallah in a small shtetl (town) in Russia. She had long, thick, black hair that she wore in two braids. Her eyes were brown and bright. She had a small, pretty mouth and a gentle smile. Her voice was soft and kind. Everybody liked Zlata. She treated her elders with respect. If someone needed a favor, Zlata was always ready to help. Her mother was a lucky woman, and Zlata gave her much nachas (joy).

When Zlata became of the right age to get married, the matchmaker in her town found her a match. The *shadchen* brought to her home a fine young man who was a good student in the Yeshiva. Zlata was very happy. He was just the kind of boy she had always hoped to marry. Everything should have been perfect, EXCEPT—

Zlata was a very, very poor girl. Her father had been a shoemaker, and when Zlata was very small, he died. There had never been any money in the house. In her whole life, Zlata had never owned a brand new dress. She always wore hand-me-downs that people brought her. Kind neighbors gave them food to eat. Sometimes Zlata's mother earned some money by helping a mother take care of a new baby. If someone was sick, Zlata's mother might help them with the housework and get some extra money. In those days things were different. Mothers did not go to work like they do today. But even if Zlata's mother worked sometimes, she never had much money.

Zlata loved her mother very much. She never complained. She tried to be happy with whatever she had.

And now, two weeks before her wedding, she sat on an old chair in the kitchen and cried and cried. It was early in the morning; it was still dark outside. Her mother had not woken up yet. Zlata had tip-toed out of the bedroom, and now she sat in the corner of the kitchen and cried so hard her whole body was shaking. She tried not to make a sound because she didn't want her mother

to know how sad she was. Her heart was broken, but Zlata was a good daughter and did not want to hurt her mother.

Zlata wanted something that she had dreamt about her whole life. Zlata wanted a brand new wedding gown. She had never cared that all her clothes were second-hand, because it did not seem that important to her. But a wedding dress—that was something else. For once in her life, she wanted a dress made especially for her.

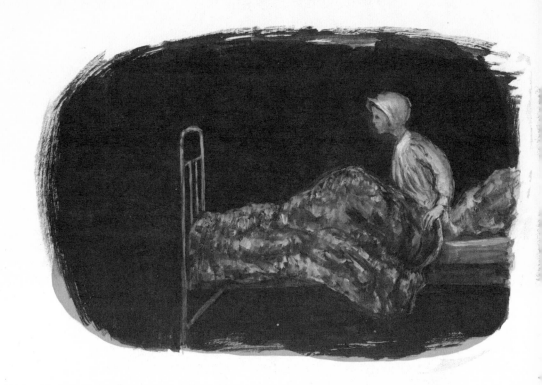

Zlata's mother woke up and heard the sobs coming from the kitchen. Tears rolled down her wrinkled old

cheeks. Her Zlata was marrying a good Jewish boy, a
yeshiva student. She had not had an easy life, but for her
goodness, she now deserved the best. Zlata needed a
wedding gown, money for a wedding feast, and some
things for her new home. Mother was very sad. It is
never easy to be poor, but at this time it was really hard.
Mother sat on the edge of the bed and cried softly. She
did not want Zlata to see her unhappiness.

Then she got an idea. True, it would break her heart,

but there was nothing else to do. She took the silver candlesticks that had belonged to her grandmother, wrapped them in a towel, and put them in her basket. This was the only valuable thing she owned, but Zlata's happiness was more important. She could use tin or iron candlesticks, but Zlata had to be happy on her wedding day!

She told Zlata that she wanted to go to the market place for a while. They had their breakfast, and then she left.

The market place was filled with people. People had come to buy or sell things. They had come from many different places with their horses and wagons. There was a lot of shouting. There is always noise and excitement at a market place. Fishermen had come to sell fish. Farmers brought fruit and vegetables. Cattle breeders came with cows, horses and chickens. Peddlers were there with aprons and kerchiefs. As soon as they had sold their goods, the people walked around to see what they could buy. Some people traded things. Everyone loved market days, that is for sure.

Zlata's mother did not quite know what to do. She stood by herself, off to the side.

A man had come to market with a pocketful of

money. He had saved up the money for a long time and
had now gone to market to try his luck in business. His
father had been a diamond dealer, and he had come to
market to buy some precious stones.

Suddenly, he noticed the woman with the basket
standing all alone. She looked so sad, as if the world was

coming to an end. He looked more closely and saw tears
rolling down her dry, wrinkled cheeks. The young man
went to her and asked her what was troubling her. It was
hard for Zlata's mother to speak. She felt choked by her
tears. Finally, in a very low voice, almost like a whisper,
she told him about Zlata's wedding and that they had no

money. There was no money for a wedding gown, no money for a wedding feast, and no money for all the things a bride needs to make a new home. She also told him that the only treasure she owned, her grandmother's silver candlesticks, were hidden in her basket. She hoped to sell them so that there would be some money for Zlata's wedding.

The bundle of money in the young man's pocket suddenly seemed very heavy. He had worked hard for a long time to save up that money. He thought for a moment. Then, without saying a word, he took the whole bundle of money and handed it to Zlata's mother. He walked away quickly into the crowd, before Zlata's mother had a chance to thank him. Zlata's mother was speechless. Her heart was filled with joy. Father in Heaven had heard their cry and now He had helped them. Zlata would have her brand new gown. Zlata would have all the things a bride needs. Now they could look forward to a beautiful, gay wedding.

The young man had not a single penny left. There was nothing for him to do at the market place, so he decided to return home. On the way, a stranger stopped him and greeted him warmly as if he had known him for years. He opened up a cloth bag he had kept hidden in his pocket and offered the young man some beautiful diamonds for a very cheap price. The young man looked at the diamonds. They were perfect stones that sparkled in brilliant colors in the sunlight. It was just what he had wanted to buy when he came to the market that day. He shook his head sadly and told the stranger, "I would have been very happy to buy these diamonds. But now I have no money. It will take me a long time to save enough money to buy any diamonds. I am sorry, but I cannot do business with you now."

The stranger did not seem surprised. He said, "Don't worry. That does not matter. I know you are a fine and

kind young man. I will trust you. Take these diamonds
and sell them. Then you can pay me back. You will find
me in the shul—in the Beth Hamidrash. Here you are,
and a good day to you." The stranger handed him the
bag with the diamonds and quickly disappeared.

50

The young man knew many diamond dealers. He sold the stones without any trouble and earned a lot of money. He was very happy and excited. As fast as he could, he went to the Beth Hamidrash to pay the stranger that had given him the diamonds on credit. The stranger was not there. He looked everywhere in the town, but there was no sign of him. The stranger had disappeared.

The young man carefully put the money aside. Later, when he counted it, he found that the profit he had made was ten times the sum of money he had given Zlata's mother. And from that day on, he was always successful in his business.

This was his reward for fulfilling the Mitzvah of Hachnosas Kallah. The Mitzvah of helping a poor girl with a dowry for the wedding is a very important Mitzvah. The young man had been kind and had given his money to Zlata's mother so that Zlata could be married in joy. And after he became a rich, important diamond merchant, he always gave money for charity, and especially for Hachnosas Kallah.

And Zlata? She danced for joy when her mother showed her the bundle of money. She clapped her hands and sang and danced all through their little house. On her wedding day, she looked very beautiful in her new, white wedding gown. The guests had never seen such a happy wedding. They danced and ate and sang a whole night.

And in Zlata's new little home, there were new dishes, shiny pots and pans, thick feather quilts, feather pillows, sheets and towels and many other things young

married people need. Her husband continued to study Torah and they lived happily ever after, and had many good Jewish children. And Zlata's mother? Every Friday night, when she *benched licht*—(lit the candles)—she thought of the kind young man, and the memory always made her smile happily.

If you ever will be asked to give money for a poor girl who is getting married, I am sure you will be happy to do your share. The Mitzvah of Hachnosas Kallah is indeed a beautiful Mitzvah, don't you agree?

THE LITTLE TYRANT

 NCE upon a time, there was a melamed, a teacher, named Reb Nissan, who lived in a small town in Russia. He was a very learned man, and also a very good and kind man. He liked all the little children in the Cheder where he taught. He liked animals and birds and all the creatures G-d had made.

His favorite pet was a rooster. The rooster was his alarm clock that woke him up every morning in time to go to "daven." At night the rooster slept inside the house near the oven, where it was warm and dry. He always got plenty to eat and the best of care. The louder the rooster crowed, the more pleased was Reb Nissan.

Yitzchak Saul, Reb Nissan's son, did not like that

rooster. He annoyed the rooster all the time, that is when-
ever his father was out of sight. He chased the rooster all
over the yard and tried to kick him when he could.

Not only did he hate the rooster, but Yitzchak Saul
hated all animals. He was a mean and wicked boy. The
hens in the barnyard laid eggs. They hatched the eggs,
they sat on them to keep them warm, and after three
weeks the cutest, fluffiest, little yellow chickens came out
of those eggs. Everyone loved those sweet little baby
chicks. Everyone, that is, except Yitzchak Saul. He threw
little stones at them and scared them. Poor little chicks.

They were so frightened, they ran all over the yard.

Sometimes he caught flies and put them inside a spider's web and watched them struggle for their life. He liked to pull the wings off insects or catch butterflies in nets. If he could get a dog to chase a cat, he was really happy. Yitzchak Saul was a cruel little boy who enjoyed hurting poor animals and creatures.

One day when Yitzchak Saul was in the yard throwing stones at birds, his father saw him. Reb Nissan became very angry. He said, "So this is the way you spend your time! I could never imagine that my own son could be so cruel and heartless!"

Yitzchak Saul looked at his father's angry face and grew frightened. His father had never seemed so upset. In the Cheder, the children respected his father, and he never had to punish them. He would scold them or give them a stern look, and that would be enough to stop any troublemaker. Yitzchak Saul had never been punished by his father, who looked very serious this time.

He called his son to come into the house with him. He opened the "Gemara Shabbos" to page one hundred and twenty-five, and read aloud the Mishnah about lowering a basket for little chicks to go out or come in so that they would not hurt themselves by having to jump a distance. "See," he said, "how the Torah thinks of everything, to make sure that little chicks are given gentle care until they are big enough to manage on their own."

Reb Nissan then turned to "Berochos" on page forty, and found the saying, "I shall give grass in your field for your animals," and after that, "and you shall eat and be satisfied." That means that first the animals should be fed and taken care of. Only then can we think of our own needs. The helpless animals that are G-d's creation should be first in our thoughts.

The father spoke in a very sad voice to his son. Not only had the boy forgotten to care for animals, but he had been cruel and mean. He was so ashamed, he kept looking at the floor. He could not lift up his head to look at his father. His father then slapped him hard.

That was the first and last time in his life that Yitzchak Saul was hit by his father. His father told him that this way he would remember the pain of the animals that he had hurt.

Yitzchak Saul cried at the punishment, but it did not hurt him as much as what happened afterwards.

Reb Nissan left his son and went into another room. Soon, Yitzchak Saul could hear his father crying behind the closed door. It sounded as if his heart was breaking, because Reb Nissan was such a good and kind man, and never could hurt anyone. Yitzchak Saul's meanness had forced his father to become so angry that he had to hit his son. Even though it hurt Reb Nissan to act in this manner, he had to teach Yitzchak Saul that cruelty is not the way of a Jewish child.

Yitzchak Saul cried and cried because he had hurt his dear father. Parents always feel sad, you know, when their children do something wrong. Parents do not like to punish their children, but to teach them right from wrong, it is sometimes necessary. Now Yitzchak Saul did not feel sorry about the punishment which he deserved, but he cried because he had made his father unhappy.

The next few days Yitzchak Saul was very quiet and

sad. On the third day, he asked his father to please for-
give him. There were tears rolling down his cheeks, and
it was hard for him to talk.

Reb Nissan's eyes filled with tears as he held his son
in a warm hug. He told him that it was not so serious

because he was still a little boy, but he did not want him to grow up and become a cold-hearted, unfeeling person.

From that day, Yitzchak Saul was a different boy. He never again was cruel to animals. He never again even wanted to hurt any animals. He changed so much, it was hard to believe that he had ever been such a thoughtless, bad boy. Yitzchak Saul had learned his lesson well.

[This story was taken from the "Memoirs" of Rabbi Joseph I. Schneersohn, of saintly memory, a world famous Jewish leader.]